WALT DISNEY'S

Song
of the
South

Based on Walt Disney Company's
full-length feature film

This adaptation by
Victoria Crenson

TROLL ASSOCIATES

Chapter One

The carriage rattled along the dusty road. The horses were tired after their long journey. Now they were slowing down, almost as if they recognized the plantation as the end of their long haul.

Inside the carriage young Johnny looked across at his mother and father, and then at Tempy, their faithful servant who dozed in the corner. They were all tired, and nobody had spoken for the past hour. It was hot. Too hot.

"Mama," Johnny broke the long silence. "Why are we going to Grandma's?"

Sally, his mother thought for a minute. "Well, I told you... just a ... visit."

"Why don't she come to see us like she did last spring?" He had an uneasy feeling that his parents were not telling him the real reason why they had made the long trip out to the plantation.

"Well," said Sally, "I thought that you'd ...enjoy seeing the plantation."

"Is Grandma mad at us?"

Johnny's question took his mother by surprise. "Why, no! Of course not, Johnny," she said. "Whatever gave you that idea?"

"Well, Georgie says everybody's mad at what Daddy writes in the newspaper!" He looked at his father, but he did not seem to have heard. "Don't Grandma read the newspaper?"

"She does! And she likes what's in it!"

John, his father, had an angry expression on his face and, noticing this, Johnny was silent again. He wished that he knew just what they had come here for. But they weren't going to tell him the real reason. There was nothing else to do but to wait and see.

"Gracious! We're almost there!" The slowing down of the carriage had awakened Tempy. "You ain't never heard frogs like these in Atlanta. Listen to what they're saying! 'Knee-deep! Knee-deep!' I remember the time, young Johnny, when your father caught a whole box of them and they got loose in your grandma's milk-house. I remember," she grinned, "what your Daddy got for doin' it, too!"

"Well, it was old Uncle Remus's fault. He told me that story about Brer Frog." Johnny's father laughed as he remembered the days of his boyhood. "The tale about him having a tail and how he lost it!"

Then everybody laughed; that made Johnny feel a lot easier.

"Is Uncle Remus real?" he asked.

"Real? Of course he's real," said Tempy. "You just wait 'til you hear him tell a tale about Brer Rabbit. Then you'll know he's real!"

The carriage had come to a stop. Some children came to greet the passengers. Then a smiling woman appeared in the doorway - Doshy, Johnny's grandmother.

"You get more like your grandfather every time I see you," she said to Johnny. "Welcome home," she said to the others.

One of the children who had come to greet the visitors was a boy Johnny's age named Toby. Right away Johnny made friends with him.

"Come on, Johnny," said Toby. "I'll show you the big Grandpa clock."

As they went inside, the door swung partly open and while Toby chattered, Johnny listened to what the adults were saying outside on the porch. Doshy was talking to Johnny's father in a stern voice.

"A fine lot o' trouble you've been causing in Atlanta," she scolded. "Thumping for cotton mills, railways, and heaven knows what!"

Johnny couldn't hear the reply. After a little while Johnny heard his father talking to his mother in a much louder voice.

"Well, what are you going to tell her? Have you changed your mind, or are you still going to stay?"

"Oh, I have to stay, John," Sally sounded sad but determined. "It wouldn't be fair to Mama. She has enough responsibility, and I'm not going to saddle her with ours."

"But it's only for a short time. She'd be only too glad to take care of Johnny."

Johnny felt a sinking feeling in his stomach. His father was going away... maybe his mother, too. He heard his grandmother join his parents on the porch.

"Sally wants Johnny to stay here with you for a while," he heard his father say.

"And what are you going to do meanwhile?" asked Doshy.

"Oh, I'm going back, and I want Sally to go with me!"

"It's no use, John," said Sally close to tears. "I'm not going back."

"Then I'll go without you." His father seemed to have made a final decision. "I'll have to hurry or I'll miss my train!"

Johnny could hold himself back no longer. He rushed out the door and flung his arms around his father's waist. "Daddy, you're... you're going back?"

"Yes, son, I'm afraid I am. I have to."

"But you've never left Mama and me before!"

"I've got a job to do, Johnny," his voice

was husky. "So have you. You've got to take care of your mother and your grandmother. You'll do that for me, won't you?" He stooped and kissed Johnny.

"Goodbye, Sally."

Johnny turned his head away. It always embarrassed him when his parents kissed. There was a lump in his throat and now he couldn't hold back the tears. He saw his father walking back to the carriage. The wheels rumbled forward, and then the horses picked up speed.

Johnny just stood there, the tears streaming down his face. His mother knelt beside him.

"Don't cry, Johnny," her voice was shaky and he knew it was hard for her to keep a brave face. "He'll be back...someday!"

Panic flooded over him. He rushed down the wooden steps into the dusty road. The carriage was almost out of sight now, a small cloud of dust on the far horizon.

"Daddy! Daddy!" he sobbed. " Come back! I won't stay here! If you go I'm going, too!"

It was no good. The carriage was now out

of sight and already the dust was beginning to settle.

Johnny cried into his pillow that night. His father was gone. How long would he be away? He might never see him again! He wished that he was old enough to understand what the grownups had been talking about.

Suddenly, he had an idea and he stopped crying. He wondered why he hadn't thought about it before. He would follow after his father. Not in the panic-stricken way he had rushed after the carriage that day but, instead, by carefully tracking him. It wouldn't be easy, but he would keep going, sleeping under the giant cottonwood trees when he was tired. He would press on until at last he found his father. Then he would persuade him to come back.

He got out of bed and quietly began to dress. A few minutes later he was on the verandah, his small pack on his back. A full moon shone overhead, and the plantation was bathed in its silvery glow. Ahead of him lay the rough dusty road that his father had taken. Without stopping for a moment he set off.

He crossed the small wooden bridge, the water sparkling below him, and began to walk faster. He had no idea how long it would take him to find his father, but even if he couldn't find him, he would not return. He would wander on alone for the rest of his days, leaving his troubles behind him.

This is what he was thinking about when he first heard the singing. It was coming from some trees on his left.

He left the road and followed the sound. A few minutes later, peering from behind a large cottonwood tree, he saw a group of people singing around a campfire.

One voice in particular caught his attention. The man was sitting with his back to Johnny, but he knew right away who it was - Uncle Remus himself! Then he saw Toby.

"Uncle Remus," said Toby, "you tell the best tales in the whole United States of Georgia!"

Uncle Remus looked in Johnny's direction

but he gave no sign that he had noticed him hiding behind the tree.

Suddenly he heard another familiar voice. It was Tempy!

Chapter Two

Tempy stepped into the clearing. "Miss Sally's been lookin' high and low for young Johnny." Tempy looked at Uncle Remus suspiciously. "You sure he ain't been down here listening to one of your tales?"

"Course he isn't. Wouldn't I have seen him?" It was Toby who answered her.

Uncle Remus stood up and pushed his hat to the back of his head.

"You tell Miss Sally the boy's with me. Tell her not to worry," he said.

"What d'you mean he's with you?" Tempy stood with her hands on her hips, a look of anger on her face.

"Never mind," Uncle Remus smiled. "Just tell her what I say. Now go on, Tempy. Off you go!"

As soon as Tempy had left the clearing, Uncle Remus turned and began walking towards Johnny's hiding place. Suddenly Johnny felt like running. Uncle Remus, kind as he was, would only take him back to his mother. Then he would never find his father. Johnny turned and began to run, back into the deep woods. Briars tore at his arms and legs, his heart was pounding and he didn't know where he was heading. All he wanted to do was get far away from his troubles.

Then his foot caught in a gnarled root and he fell headlong. He dragged himself to his feet and sat down on a fallen tree trunk. In his heart he knew that he could go no further. He would never be able to find his father. Sinking his head into his hands, he burst into tears. Johnny heard Uncle Remus's footsteps, but he did not look up. He would be taken back, and that would be that.

Uncle Remus lowered himself down beside Johnny, and began wiping the boy's eyes with his handkerchief.

"Well, bless my soul!" he smiled comfortingly. "You've gone and got somethin' in your eye, and I ain't surprised, runnin' through the woods like that."

Uncle Remus picked up the small backpack. "Appears to me like you're goin' somewhere," he said.

"I am, and nobody's gonna stop me!" Johnny snapped.

Uncle Remus stroked his beard. "You know, I was just figgerin' on doing something like that myself. How'd you like ol' Uncle Remus to go along with you?"

Johnny stood up and looked at the man. "I'm going to Atlanta!" he said standing very straight.

"Hmm," Uncle Remus looked down at him.

"It's a powerful long walk to Atlanta!" He looked in Johnny's bag. "You bring some grub?" he asked.

"No," Johnny admitted feeling foolish.

"S'pose we stop by my place and pick some up," said Uncle Remus.

Johnny nodded and fell into step beside his new friend. Already things were looking up. He was going away from all his troubles, and with luck he might find his father. If he didn't, then at least he'd have Uncle Remus.

They walked on until they came to Uncle Remus' cabin. It was spick and span inside and the smell of woodsmoke hung in the air.

"Sort of late in the day to be startin' on such a long trip, ain't it?" Uncle Remus remarked as he closed the door.

"Well, you don't have to go just 'cause you said you would." Johnny felt that maybe his friend was backing down at the last minute. Perhaps it had been a trick to keep him from setting out in the first place.

"I ain't said nothin' about not goin'," said Uncle Remus. " 'Cause I'll go."

"And I'm not coming back!" Johnny added.

Uncle Remus chuckled, and set about roasting some potatoes in the embers of the dying fire.

"You're laughing at me!" Johnny accused.

"No sir!" said Uncle Remus. "I'm laughing

'cause those are exactly the words that old Brer Rabbit used the time he lit out from his briar patch! 'And I ain't never comin' back, neither!' Well," the old man said with a sigh, "I reckon I better be gettin' my things together so we can be leavin'."

Johnny stood and watched as Uncle Remus packed his bag. "What did you say about Brer Rabbit?" he blurted out. "You said there was a tale about Brer Rabbit not coming back to his briar patch. Please tell me, Uncle Remus."

"Well," Uncle Remus began, "you just listen with both ears wide open 'cause Brer Rabbit he's the out-doin'est, the most bodacious critter in the whole world. Now this tale didn't happen just yesterday nor the day before. T'was a long time ago in the days where everything was mighty satisfactual. The critters in those days were closer to the folks, and it was a lot, lot better world all around. It happened on one of them 'Zip-a-dee-doo-dah' days. Now that's the kind of a day when you can't open your mouth without a song jumpin' right out of it..."

With that, Uncle Remus burst into song:

Zip-a-dee-doo-dah, zip-a-dee-day
My, oh my, what a beautiful day,
Plenty of sunshine headin' my way,
Zip-a-dee-doo-dah, zip-a-dee-day...

As Johnny listened, it seemed that he was no longer in that cabin. Blue skies were up above, blossoms were falling like a shower of April snow, birds were singing,

18

and butterflies were fluttering all around.

They walked on through the warm, sunlit woods, Uncle Remus singing and Johnny following until they heard a sudden hammering. Ahead of them was a rabbit who was busily nailing boards across the door of his house. He was muttering to himself and seemed to be in a very bad mood.

"Doggone ol' briar patch!" mumbled Brer Rabbit giving the last nail a final bang.

"I'm goin' to leave this ol' place...for good... and I ain't never comin' back!"

"You mean you're goin' to leave the briar patch, the place where you were born and raised?" asked Uncle Remus.

"That I is!" said Brer Rabbit giving the nail another whack, but instead he brought the hammer down on his thumb. "Ow!" he shrieked. "See what I mean? That old briar patch ain't brought nothin' but trouble. This is where my trouble is, so this is the place I'm getting away from!"

"Don't you know you can't run away from trouble? There ain't no place that far," replied Uncle Remus solemnly.

"Well just the same, I've made up my mind, and I ain't never comin' back."

Johnny and Uncle Remus watched Brer Rabbit hop away. Uncle Remus chuckled almost as if he knew what would happen next!

Chapter Three

They watched Brer Rabbit for some time, the 'zip-a-dee' song growing fainter all the while.

Then, suddenly, before their very eyes, he seemed to take off into the air, catapulting into space, and then he was dangling in the branches of a tree. He was caught in a sapling trap! Johnny gasped but Uncle Remus only chuckled.

"There he dangled, twixt the heavens and the earth. First he's scared he's goin' to fall...he yanked and he pulled and he heaved and he hauled, but t'was no use. He knows somebody's caught him all right and he knows who that somebody is. Sure enough, up on Chickapin Hill..."

Johnny saw the fox looking out from the

bottom of a tree trunk. He knew his trap had been sprung because of the ringing of the cowbell attached to the sapling trap.

"Old Brer Fox," Uncle Remus went on, "he knows he done caught old Brer Rabbit. 'I got that old Brer Rabbit at last! Heh!' And he grabs his axe and makes ready to settle Brer Rabbit's hash."

Johnny watched as Brer Rabbit, finally worn out by his struggles, lay still.

"Now Brer Rabbit ain't got much strength so he got to use his head," Uncle Remus continued. "And that's exactly what he started to do when he heard old Brer Bear come ambling down the road. Brer Bear was singing, too, 'Zip-a-dee-doo-dah, zip-a-dee-ay...'"

"How do you do, Brer Bear," Brer Rabbit said.

Brer Bear looked startled. Looking up he saw Brer Rabbit dangling above him. His eyes nearly popped out of his head. "What you doin' up there?" he growled.

Brer Rabbit smiled as though there was nothing strange about hanging up in the tree. "Oh, keepin' the crows outa the cornfield. I make a dollar a minute."

Brer Bear gulped. "A dollar a minute!" he gasped.

"Indeed I am," said Brer Rabbit. "Would you like to make a dollar a minute, Brer Bear?"

"Yeah, but..." Brer Bear was greedy, yet suspicious. Was this one of Brer Rabbit's tricks?

"You'd make a mighty fine scarecrow, Brer Bear," Brer Rabbit continued, smiling. "How'd you like the job?"

"Oh yeah, sure!" Brer Bear scratched his head. "But I couldn't take it away from you."

Meanwhile, Brer Fox, holding his axe and grinning, was hurrying down the hill towards the trapped rabbit.

"You take the job, Brer Bear," said Brer Rabbit trying not to sound panicked. "I've got other things I've gotta do!"

"Oh well," Brer Bear finally made up his mind. "I'll take the job. Thanks, Brer Rabbit!" They shook hands. As Brer

Rabbit took Brer Bear's hand he gave a mighty tug and broke free of the sapling trap. "I'm sure mighty grateful," said Brer Bear still shaking hands. All this time Brer Fox was getting closer, laughing to himself. This was too good to be true. He licked his lips as he thought about the tasty meal Brer Rabbit would make.

Brer Rabbit pulled his hand free and, grabbing his bundle, hopped off behind some nearby rocks. "So long, Brer Bear," he called.

Lucky Brer Bear climbed up into the sapling already thinking of the money he was going to make. It was very strange that there were no crows around, but that would make his job easier. "Dollar a minute...zip-a-dee-ay," he sang softly to himself when suddenly, Brer Fox appeared.

"What you doin' there? Get out of my trap!" he snarled.

"Zip-a-dee.." Brer Bear was not going to give up his dollar-a-minute job for anybody, not even Brer Fox.

Brer Fox swung his axe and sliced right through the sapling. With an ear-splitting crack, Brer Bear came crashing down right on top of Brer Fox.

Brer Bear grabbed Brer Fox, picked him up and blew the dust off him. "Now what's the game?" growled Brer Bear. "I was makin' a dollar a minute until you came along !"

"You was not makin' a dollar a minute," Brer Fox replied. "You was makin' a fool of yourself!"

Brer Bear tightened his grip on Brer Fox, pulling him up until their faces were inches apart. Meanwhile, Brer Rabbit was on top of a large rock, jumping up and down with glee at the sight of Brer Bear and Brer Fox arguing. "Hit him in the mouth, Brer Fox," he cried. "Clip him in the head, Brer Bear!"

The fox and the bear turned around.

"Look at that rabbit!" screeched Brer Fox. "He made a fool out of you, you fool!"

"He did?" Brer Bear was just beginning to realize that maybe Brer Rabbit had tricked him again. Brer Bear was getting angry. "In that case..." Brer Bear knocked Brer Fox to one side. "Let me at 'im!"

"You keep out of this, Brer Bear," Brer Fox snarled, picking himself up. "He's mine!"

Brer Rabbit decided it was time to leave. He turned to run, but his head hit an overhanging piece of rock and knocked him over backwards. All he could see in front of his eyes were stars.

Brer Fox was the first to grab Brer Rabbit. "He's mine! I caught him!"

"He's mine!" roared Brer Bear grabbing Brer Fox. Together they rolled over, in the dust snarling and fighting. Once more Brer Rabbit squirmed his way out and under cover of the rising dust, ran to freedom.

"Brer Rabbit was well on his way," concluded Uncle Remus. "He took his foot in his hand, and lit out for home where he belonged. Just like I told him in the first place, you can't run away from trouble. There ain't no place that far!"

Johnny suddenly came back to reality. He was sitting in Uncle Remus's cabin. He found it hard to believe that he had never been away from that fireside.

"Where's Brer Rabbit's briar patch?" he asked. "Do you think we could find it?"

"Course we could," Uncle Remus' eyes twinkled. "But what's the use of speculatin' on that when we're goin' away?"

Johnny dropped his head and thought awhile. "Do you think we ought to go, Uncle Remus?" he asked.

"Not go?" Uncle Remus slapped his thigh. "After I went and fixed all this grub? What's come over you?"

"Well...Brer Rabbit..."

"What's Brer Rabbit got to do with this? And just when I was getting a hankerin' to go."

"Well, if you really want to go, Uncle Remus..." said Johnny half-heartedly.

"Oh, never mind," said Uncle Remus with a smile. "I can give it up if you can."

Johnny was relieved. Only a short time ago nothing would have stopped him from leaving. Now, he did not want to go. Maybe Brer Rabbit had been right. You just can't run away from trouble, because there is nowhere that far away.

Chapter Four

"Uncle Remus!" shouted Toby from outside the cabin. Johnny rushed across the room and hid behind a chair. The door opened and in came Toby with a worried look on his face. "Uncle Remus, I can't find Johnny anywhere, and I'm supposed to be lookin' after him. I reckon he's done for!" Toby was close to tears. "He mighta got himself lost! He mighta fallen in the mill pond! He mighta got eaten up!"

Suddenly Johnny burst out laughing.

"Why, it's him!" Toby gasped.

"Maybe it's just his ghost!" laughed Uncle Remus.

"It's him, alright. He's sure gonna catch it when he gets home!"

"I guess I better take my foot in my hand

and get going, Uncle Remus," said Johnny feeling that the sooner he got it over with the better.

"Hold on there!" Uncle Remus stood up and reached for his hat. "I reckon you'd better let old Uncle Remus go with you."

Johnny's mother, Tempy and Doshy were waiting anxiously on the verandah for news of Johnny when they spied Uncle Remus and the two boys coming down the road. Everybody stood back as Johnny approached his mother.

"Johnny! Where have you been?" His mother's voice was stern, but she was also very relieved to see him.

"Miss Sally," said Uncle Remus stepping forward. "Didn't Tempy tell you he was with me?"

"Yes, she told me," said Sally, "but it's so long past Johnny's bedtime."

"It was my fault," Uncle Remus apologized. "I was telling him a tale about Brer Rabbit, and I plum forgot the time."

"Well, I don't mind you telling him stories, Uncle Remus, but you know perfectly well it's too late for him to be up."

"Yes, ma'am," said Uncle Remus. "It won't happen again."

Johnny and his mother disappeared inside. "Miss Doshy," said Uncle Remus. "What that child need is his pa."

"And that's what his mother needs, too," Doshy sighed, "but I'm afraid it's going to take a little while for her to find that out."

"You ain't mad with me, are you?" asked Uncle Remus.

"You meddling old rascal," Doshy laughed. "Of course I'm not mad with you."

Uncle Remus smiled and turning around, he went back to his cabin.

Early the next morning, Johnny and Toby decided to go looking for Brer Frog down by the millpond.

"How far is it?" asked Johnny.

"Oh, not far. Over there around the bend," said Toby. They walked on and Johnny was just about to climb over the first fence they came to when Toby pulled him back. "You can't cut across there!"

"Why not?" Johnny was puzzled.

"That's why!" Toby pointed to a huge bull no more than twenty yards away. It snorted and pawed the ground. "Sure is lucky I was with you!"

They made a detour and crossed the river by the footbridge. On their right was a small house and as they passed they heard a puppy crying. Johnny stopped.

"Them two," Toby nodded towards two boys and a girl who stood a short distance away. "Them boys are bad 'uns. Joe and Jake. That's Ginny with 'em."

The boys were arguing with Ginny over the puppy. "We ought to drown him," Joe sneered.

"Sure. He's the runt," Jake agreed.

"This here's my puppy!" Ginny wailed. "You leave him alone!"

"Oh, go on, Ginny. Ha! Ha!" Jake teased.

Toby looked at Johnny. "Those are the Favers boys," he whispered. "My ma don't allow me to play with them. Your ma won't either if she catches you."

Suddenly the puppy broke free and ran to

Johnny and Toby. Toby picked it up and it nestled in his arms.

Already Joe and Jake were climbing over the fence and rushing up to Toby. They grabbed the pup from him. "Let go of him before I knock your head clean off!" Joe snarled. Then he turned to Johnny. "Where'd you get the funny-lookin' clothes? Look at that lace collar."

"Look at the little girlie," Jake sneered.

Toby pulled Johnny away and with the shouts of Jake and Joe ringing in their ears, they headed towards the millpond.

They were surprised when Ginny came out of the trees, clutching the puppy to her with a worried look on her face. "You can have my puppy," she said handing him to Johnny. "For keeps, if you'll be nice to him. His name is Teenchy. They were going to drown him."

"Gee, he's beautiful!" said Johnny.

Their frog hunting forgotten, Johnny and Toby set off back home.

Chapter Five

When Tempy caught sight of the puppy she called, "You take that puppy right back where you found him. And don't waste any time about it either."

Johnny looked down at the puppy. He knew that he could never part with it. "You're my puppy, and that's all there is to it," he murmured. There was only one person who would see his point of view. He set off for Uncle Remus's cabin.

"Well bless my soul!" said Uncle Remus "Ain't that one of the Faverses' dogs? You been playin' with those boys?"

"No, Uncle Remus," said Johnny.

"You'd better tote that right back where it came from."

"But Uncle Remus, Ginny gave him to me," pleaded Johnny.

"What's your ma gonna say. She's not gonna let you keep him."

"Maybe not in the house," said Johnny.

"But suppose you kept him for me, Uncle Remus!"

"Now hold on there!" Uncle Remus was shocked. "You don't really expect old Uncle Remus to keep that dog for you. Where am I going to get the stuff to feed him with? He'd be up half the night hollerin' and I'd be up outa bed lettin' him in and lettin' him out...Course, I don't expect a little dog like that would eat very much. And it ain't like you can't get used to a little hollerin' and I got a corner that ain't bein' used."

"Oh, Uncle Remus! " Johnny cried. The puppy wriggled from Johnny's arms into Uncle Remus's outstretched hands.

"Look at that!" A broad grin spread across Uncle Remus's face. "Doggone if he don't act like he thinks I'm gonna keep him."

Johnny followed Uncle Remus into the cabin. Soon Toby arrived. It looked like everything was going to work out fine until Johnny and Toby heard voices when they were walking home. "That's those Favers boys!" gasped Toby. "They're out to make trouble. They want the dog back. We'd better get back to Uncle Remus's right away."

But by the time they arrived back at the clearing, Jake and Joe Favers and a group of their friends were standing around the cabin; Uncle Remus stood in the doorway.

"Stop pesterin' me, boys," Uncle Remus said. "Ain't no 'if s' and 'buts' about it. I ain't gonna give you the dog unless Johnny tells me to. He's Johnny's dog."

"Ginny gave him to me," said Johnny.

"T'weren't hers to give!" spat out Jake. "That dog's ours and we're going to take him."

"If I hear one more word about this puppy," Uncle Remus took a couple steps forward, "I'll..."

The boys began backing away. "We'll get him yet, you'll see!" Jake yelled. Then they left, running off into the trees.

"Johnny!" Ginny came out from the bushes where she'd been hiding. " If they give you trouble, you just tell my ma. She'll whale the daylights out of them." Then she raced away, taking a short cut that would get her home before her brothers.

Uncle Remus, Toby and Johnny went inside the cabin and closed the door. "Well," said Uncle Remus lowering himself into his favorite chair. "You're just like Brer Rabbit when he stuck his foot into somethin' he know nothin' about. You ever heard that tale?"

"Not yet, Uncle Remus," Johnny replied.

"I was goin' fishin' one morning," Uncle Remus began, "and I was just thinking how the flowers and critters was curious things. They can look in your heart and tell if it's singing. If it's whistling a song, they all say 'howdy' when you come along."

Then Brer Rabbit came hopping over the hill. Even when he stopped in front of Uncle Remus, he still hopped up and down.

"Stop jumpin, Brer Rabbit," Uncle Remus grinned. "You'll run outa breath. Why don't you sit down and calm yourself?"

"When the grasshopper jumps and so does the flea, I do what I like and I suits me!" And Brer Rabbit scampered off.

They didn't know it at the time but Brer Rabbit was heading straight for trouble, because up on Chickapin Hill, at the edge of the big woods, was where old Brer Fox lived, and Brer Fox sure hadn't forgotten their last meeting...

Chapter Six

Old Brer Fox was mighty curious about the whereabouts of old Brer Rabbit. So when he saw Brer Rabbit coming, he could hardly believe his eyes. With a snarl he dived back down into his den at the foot of the cottonwood tree. Brer Bear was in there, too, paying him a visit.

"Here he comes! Here he comes!" Brer Fox danced around with glee. Then he went across to the large pot that was bubbling over the fire.

"Now where was I? Ah, yes. The head. Gotta get a head right quick. That old rabbit won't get away this time. No siree!"

"That's what you said the last time and the time before that," Brer Bear mumbled. "Brer Rabbit's just too smart."

Brer Fox began ladling tar out of the pot and smearing it on the head of a dummy figure. Then, with a grin, he stepped back to admire his work. "I'm going to show him who the smartest is," he leered."The Tar Baby sure gonna fool him!"

"It ain't gonna fool nobody." said Brer Bear. "It ain't got no eyes." Brer Fox pulled two buttons off Brer Bear's coat and stuck them on the face of the dummy. He took the bowl of Brer Bear's pipe and stuck it on for the nose. Then he yanked a bunch of

hair off Brer Bear's back and stuck it on the dummy's head.

"Come on, come on, Brer Bear," urged Brer Fox. "We've got to hurry. That rabbit's comin' down the road now!" Together they carried the tar figure to the side of the road. "He'll be along here in just a minute and everything has to be just right. Say, this Tar Baby could use a hat." The fox grabbed the bear's hat and put it on the dummy's head.

"Look at that rascal scamperin' down the road!" muttered Brer Fox as he dove for cover. "I'll fix 'im. I'll kill 'im."

"How do you do?" Brer Rabbit pulled up in front of the Tar Baby. Brer Rabbit was puzzled. He thought the Tar Baby was very rude not to reply.

"How do you do?" he said for a second time. There was no reply. He scratched his head with his left hind foot. He wanted to know why the Tar Baby was not answering him. He looked the dummy over.

"What's the matter with you?" he asked. "Are you hard of hearing? I said 'howdy'!"

Behind the bushes the fox was standing on the bear's back so that he could see what was happening. "I hope it works," he said. "Ha Ha!"

By this time Brer Rabbit was becoming very angry with the rudeness of the Tar Baby. "If you don't say 'howdy' by the time I count three," he snarled, "I'm gonna bust you wide open!" Brer Rabbit started to count. "One! Two!" Brer Rabbit paused. It didn't look like the Tar Baby was going to reply and he really didn't want to hit him. "Two and a half! Three! Take that!"

Brer Rabbit's fist was stuck fast in the tar. No matter how much he tried, he couldn't get it free. "Turn me loose!" he wailed. "Or I'll poke you again. Let me go!"

Now Brer Rabbit kicked into the side of the Tar Baby. His foot stuck and he fell forward. Soon he was completely covered in tar kicking and screaming until he was so stuck up that he could hardly move his eyeballs. He was a helpless prisoner. It was with fear in his heart that he saw Brer Bear and Brer Fox come out from where

they had been hiding.

"How do you do?" Brer Fox smiled. Brer Fox poked the rabbit on the nose. "You are a pretty smart feller," he jeered, "but the business you mind the best is your own. Folks say Brer Rabbit knows a lot of tricks, but he forgot them today."

Brer Fox and Brer Bear began dancing around the trapped rabbit. Brer Rabbit had learned his lesson too late...

Uncle Remus paused to light his pipe. Johnny and Toby were close to tears thinking that this was the end of Brer Rabbit. But Uncle Remus continued...

It looked like the finish of Brer Rabbit, lying helpless in the tar, at the mercy of Brer Fox and Brer Bear. They were already planning to barbecue him.

"I'm gonna stay for dinner," said Brer Bear, "but first I'm gonna do what I said I would do. I'm gonna knock that rabbit's head clean off!"

"No!No!"Brer Fox shrieked. "It's too quick! After all the trouble that rabbit's caused us, we want him to suffer, don't we?"

"Brer Bear," the rabbit squealed, "Please knock my head clean off. Don't let Brer Fox fling me into that briar patch!"

"Maybe I'll hang you instead," snarled Brer Fox.

"Then hang me!" said Brer Rabbit. "Skin me alive, just please don't throw me in that briar patch!"

A gleam appeared in the fox's eyes. "Did you say 'briar patch' Brer Rabbit?"

"No! No! Please...not in there!" Brer Rabbit screamed. Brer Fox threw Brer Rabbit

high into the air above the wicked-looking briar patch.

"That rabbit will be ripped to pieces now!" said Brer Fox. He and Brer Bear smiled as they listened to Brer Rabbit thrashing about and screaming.

Suddenly they heard a peal of laughter from the brambles. "Here I am, Brer Fox," Brer Rabbit laughed. "I was born and bred in the briar patch!"

Uncle Remus laughed. "Old Brer Fox and Brer Bear knew they'd been beat again."

Chapter Seven

Johnny and Toby left the cabin and headed home. But Jake and Joe Favers had not gone home. The two bullies stepped out from the bushes where they had been laying in wait.

"Just cause old Remus takes your side," Jake sneered, "don't mean we ain't gonna get that pup. We're gonna tell on you. We're gonna tell Tempy!"

"Go ahead!" Johnny snapped. "You can tell my ma and Aunt Tempy for all I care! But whatever you do, don't tell your ma."

"Isn't that what Brer Rabbit did to Brer Fox?" Toby whispered.

"Being little, we're supposed to use our heads and our feet!" Johnny replied.

"We're goin straight back to tell our ma!"

said Jake. The Favers boys marched away.

As Johnny and Toby passed the Faverses' house, they saw Jake and Joe run out holding their backsides. Ma Favers appeared on the porch holding a stick.

"That's Ginny's dog," she yelled. "And if she wants to give it away, it's none of your business!"

"That Johnny thinks he's so smart!" said Jake. "We'll get him and the dog!"

The next day at the plantation Tempy and Uncle Remus were in the kitchen when they heard the voices of the Favers boys calling from the yard.

"What do you boys want?" asked Tempy coming to the door.

"We want to speak to Miss Sally," said Joe.

"Don't you know that Miss Sally's got no time to be bothered with you. And she don't want to hear anymore about that mangy dog, either," said Uncle Remus.

"What's this all about?" said Miss Sally coming to the door. The boys told her about the puppy and how Uncle Remus was keeping it so she wouldn't know. She told Uncle Remus to return the puppy to the Favers.

"Miss Sally," said Uncle Remus, "Johnny didn't mean no harm. He was just tryin' to be like Brer Rabbit..."

"Your stories only confuse the boy," she snapped. "From now on I don't want you to tell him anymore stories."

"Yes, ma'am," said Uncle Remus sadly as he walked away.

Doshy was upset when she heard what Sally had told Uncle Remus. "Johnny will be so unhappy without Uncle Remus's stories. The boy must have friends. That's just common sense."

"Next week is his birthday. He can have a party and invite some girls and boys," said Sally.

Johnny was excited about the party. "Gee, can I ask Ginny to come? Maybe you can write Daddy and invite him."

"I'll write and ask him," Sally replied softly.

"Oh boy!" cried Johnny as he sprinted off

to see Uncle Remus. "Uncle Remus!" He pushed open the door. "Where's Teenchy?"

"Gone! Back at the Favers' where he belongs."

"But Teenchy's mine! Ginny gave him to me and you said..."

"Never mind what I said!" Uncle Remus sounded angry. "Your ma told you to take that dog back but you didn't. She don't like that and I don't blame her."

"Jake will drown her! I know he will! You don't even care..."

"Makes no difference whether I do or don't," Uncle Remus replied. "I'm just a wornout old man that ain't no good to nobody!"

"But Uncle Remus," Johnny was fighting hard to hold back his tears, "you're the best friend I've got..."

"Maybe so," the old man's voice was shaky, "but I know this. I ain't goin' to be tellin' you anymore stories!"

Johnny walked slowly to the door, and it was only when he was outside that he finally broke down and cried.

Chapter Eight

The children flocked to Johnny's birthday party on the following Tuesday. Even the Favers children were invited. When Johnny went to her house to pick her up, Ginny was dressed in a pretty dress her mother had made for her. As they walked to the party the Favers boys walked behind teasing Ginny. Finally Jake gave her a violent push right into the mud.

"You've spoiled my dress!" cried Ginny.

Johnny was angry. He had hoped that an invitation to the party would help him to make friends with the Favers boys but now it seemed that would never be. Angrily he began swapping punches with Jake. Joe just stood back, watching and laughing. Johnny and Jake rolled on the ground

fighting furiously. Ginny, now very frightened, ran off.

Jake began to realize that things were not going his way. Slowly Johnny was getting the better of him, landing punches that really hurt.

"Ouch!" Jake called out. "Make him stop, Joe. C'mon, give me a hand!"

But Joe just walked away. He didn't want to get hurt himself. Then he saw a big stick lying by the side of the road. Holding the stick above his head, he moved in on the two boys and waited for his chance to strike a blow at Johnny that would put him out of the fight for good.

He saw his chance. He swung his weapon but he never struck the blow. The stick was pulled out of his hand and thrown far away. He found himself held in a grip from which there was no escape.

"All right," Uncle Remus ordered. "Stop fighting!" Now you two Favers get along and don't let me catch you pesterin' these children again. And I mean it!"

Ginny was crying. "Bless my soul. What's this?" said Uncle Remus.

"Ginny can't go to the party 'cause she's all dirty and I don't want to go...Daddy didn't come..."

They sat down on a log, and then Uncle Remus began to chuckle. "Course, we all got troubles, but they ain't none of us ever had troubles like poor Brer Rabbit. Yes sir, he was down there in Brer Fox's cave, and this time it looked like his time had really run out."

As Uncle Remus began his tale it seemed to Ginny and Johnny that all their troubles were far away and they were watching Brer Rabbit in the fox's lair...

Brer Rabbit was tied up to the wall of the cave and with Brer Bear licking his lips at the table, Brer Fox was making up the fire.

"You've played your last trick on me, Brer Rabbit," said the fox. He moved over and looped a length of rope around Brer Rabbit's head and tied a knot."Yes sir!" Brer Fox was really in a good mood. "He's dressed up for my dinner, all right. 'Cause I'm gonna barbecue him!"

"Ain't that awful," Brer Rabbit managed to laugh. Then he began to laugh loudly.

"Now, wait a minute." Brer Fox was getting angry at Brer Rabbit's laughter. "I said I'm gonna roast you on the fire. Is that somethin' to laugh at?"

"I can't help laughin', Brer Fox," giggled Brer Rabbit. "I just been to my Laughing Place and every time I think about it, I just can't help laughin'!"

"What's a Laughing Place?" Brer Bear was very curious indeed.

"Oh that," Brer Rabbit grinned, "is just a secret place I know about."

Brer Fox untied some of Brer Rabbit's ropes and picked him up. "You keep out of this, Brer Bear!" he snarled. "It's another one of his tricks!"

"Where is this Laughing Place?" asked Brer Bear. His curiosity was getting the better of him.

"How can I show you where it is when I'm all tied up like this?" Brer Rabbit asked.

"I'll untie you.." Brer Bear groped for the knots.

"You keep your paws off, Brer Bear," Brer Fox snapped. "He's mine and I'm gonna cook him on this fire."

Brer Bear flew into a rage. He grabbed Brer Fox around the throat. "I wanna see that Laughing Place!" he roared.

"All right," the fox gasped. "But no tricks Brer Rabbit, or else..."

Brer Rabbit laughed and sang to himself as he led Brer Fox and Brer Bear through the woods. "A Laughing Place to go, ho, ho, ho, ho!" Brer Rabbit hopped and skipped as much as the rope would allow.

"Now look here, Brer Bear," Brer Fox said. "I'm not goin' one more step. This is just another of his tricks! That rabbit's makin' a fool of you!"

"Here it is." Brer Rabbit pointed to a clump of bushes. "This is the Laughing Place."

"You go in and look then, Brer Bear," said Brer Fox, "and I'll take care of this rabbit."

"There ain't nothing in here except bees!" he growled.

Brer Fox laughed. "You sure made a fool out of yourself. I ain't never seen anybody look that silly before!"

Brer Bear sure was mad. With one paw he knocked off Brer Fox's hat and jammed the bees nest on his head. With a shriek the fox jumped up and lost his hold on Brer Rabbit who bounded away. But Brer Bear grabbed the rope and hauled him back.

"You said this was the Laughing Place, and I ain't laughin!" By this time Brer Fox had the bees nest off his head and, taking careful aim, threw it at Brer Bear. It fell right over his head.

Suddenly the air was full of angry bees. In the confusion Brer Rabbit broke free. Brer Bear and Brer Fox raced around in circles swatting the swarming bees.

"I didn't say it was your Laughing Place," yelled Brer Rabbit from a safe distance. "I said it was my Laughing Place, and I'm laughing myself silly!" Brer Rabbit just sat there on that log and laughed and laughed.

Chapter Nine

"I wish I had a Laughing Place," mumbled Johnny.

"What makes you think you don't?" Uncle Remus laughed. "Everybody's got one. The trouble is most folks don't take the time to look for it."

When Johnny and Ginny got back to the plantation house, Sally came rushing up. "Johnny! Where have you been? Just look at your clothes! The party's over...What in the world have you been doing?"

"Uncle Remus told us a story about Brer Rabbit," said Ginny excitedly. "Have you got a Laughing Place, Ma'am? Uncle Remus says everybody's got one."

It was then Sally spied Uncle Remus walking slowly down the road. He looked sad. "I'm sorry, Miss Sally," he apologized.

"From now on I want you to stay away from Johnny," said Sally.

Slowly Uncle Remus turned and walked back to his cabin. He packed his clothes in an old suitcase and looked around his cabin. His heart was heavy. "Oh I know I'm just a wornout old man that don't do nothin' but tell stories. But they ain't never harmed anybody. And if they don't do no good, how can they last so long?"

Uncle Remus was aware that the door was open and that Toby was standing in the room looking at him. "I'm going away," said Uncle Remus. "I'm goin' to Atlanta!"

Johnny wandered along the banks of the creek. He knew his mother had told him not to go to Uncle Remus's cabin, but the temptation was too great."Uncle Remus! Uncle Remus!" There was no answer. He went up to the cabin and pushed the door open. "Uncle Remus, I've found my Laughing Place. It's right here..."

The cabin was empty and Uncle Remus's things were gone, too. He knew that Uncle

Remus was not coming back.

Johnny's mother was waiting for him at the plantation house. "What's the matter, Johnny?"

"Mama," he sobbed. "He's gone! Uncle Remus is gone! Where'd he go, Mama?"

Then he saw Uncle Remus's wagon heading along the same trail his father had taken.

"Uncle Remus! Wait!" Johnny ran across the dusty road. He knew he couldn't catch up to the wagon on foot...unless he took a short cut across the fields. Without thinking he ducked under the fence. The bull struggled to his feet. It saw the boy running and then it broke into a canter, picking up speed until its hooves came drumming across the grass.

"Johnny!" he heard his mother scream.

Sally and Toby ran from the verandah but it was too late. As the bull caught him, Johnny shot high into the air and then crashed with a dull thump on to the grass. The bull snorted, pawed the ground, and prepared for its next rush.

Then it heard the approach of Sally and Toby. Toby swung a big stick. Slowly the bull backed off.

"Johnny!" Sally dropped to her knees beside the still body. She picked him up and carried him back to the house.

Johnny was aware that he was in bed, but it hurt him even to open his eyes. He just wanted to sleep. The days passed.

Toby spent most of his time on the verandah waiting and praying. One day he spied a carriage coming up the road. It was

Johnny's father. Toby ran to him.

"Toby, what is it? What's the matter?"

"It's Johnny, sir. He got hurt by that bull!"

Suddenly there was a figure in the road. It was Uncle Remus. He stood back and didn't try to come closer.

Johnny's father went to the bedroom. Johnny was lying with his eyes closed.

"Johnny," Sally leaned across the bed and whispered in his ear. "Daddy's here!"

Johnny's eyes opened but he didn't recognize his parents. "Uncle Remus," he called. "Uncle Remus! Please come back!"

Doshy left the room and went out to the porch. "Uncle Remus!" she called softly. Uncle Remus came into the house and stood by the side of the bed.

"The smoke was comin' out of the chimney and the light from the lamps was soft." Uncle Remus spoke quietly watching the boy. "Inside the house the kettle was singing over the fire. Yes sir, things were mighty satisfactual 'cause Brer Rabbit come back to his Laughing Place with the folks all around him that belong there."

Johnny's eyes flickered open. "Uncle Remus! Daddy!"

"There now son," said his father, "I'm back and I'm not going away again...and we'll have more fun than Brer Rabbit himself ever did!"

"And," his mother added, "we'll have the Laughingest Place in the whole wide world!"

Uncle Remus walked outside, followed by Doshy.

"Miss Doshy," he smiled. "Things are looking mighty satisfactual. Mighty satisfactual indeed."

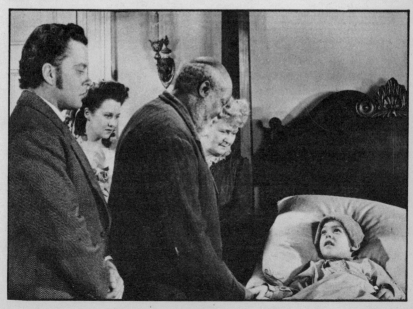